Dragon in the Cupboard

Karen Dolby

Illustrated by Caroline Church

Series Editor: Gaby Waters
Assistant Editor: Michelle Bates

Contents

About this Book

Here are George and Lottie. With tummies rumbling, they have gone to the kitchen in search of a small snack. But today everything is not quite as normal . . .

Inside the Cupboard

"Crunch . . . Crackle . . . Munch . . . Slurp . . ." The sounds were coming from a large cupboard in the farthest, darkest corner of the kitchen. Whatever could be inside?

George listened at the door and opened it quietly, just enough to peep inside. GULP! George slammed the door shut. He couldn't quite believe his eyes.

"What is it?" asked Lottie.
Trying to look bold, George grasped the
handle and this time flung open the door. There,
smiling shyly, its cheeks crammed with food was . . .

"A dragon!" gasped George.

The little dragon nodded and said, "I'm very hungry and . . . and . . . I'm lost." With that, a big tear welled up and began to trickle slowly down the creature's face.

"Please don't cry, we'll help you," said George, while Lottie patted the dragon's paw. "What happened to you?"

"Everything's mixed up and I've got a bump on my head." He gave a loud sniff and began to tell his sad tale.

The dragon's story is mixed up. Can you find out what happened to him?

What's My Name?

"The bump on your head has made you lose your memory," exclaimed Lottie. "Now we know what happened to you, we'll soon get you home," she paused. "You DO know where your home is, don't you?"

The dragon was so upset, he couldn't speak. Finally he sobbed, "No!"

Trying to cheer the dragon up and take his mind off his problems, Lottie said, "This is George and I'm Lottie. What's your name?"

The dragon wrinkled his brow. "It's . . . oh dear, I've forgotten. I know I had a badge with my name on it, but now I seem to have lost that too."

"Perhaps you dropped it," suggested George. "Let's look."

Can you spot the dragon's badge? What is his name?

Breathing Fire

Dan the dragon, was very pleased to know his name again.
"And you'll be my friends and help get me home?" he
asked. George and Lottie nodded. Dan was so excited at this
that suddenly . . . WHOOSH!

Flames shot out from the little dragon's mouth. George and Lottie leaped back in surprise as the kitchen filled with clouds of grey smoke.

"Whoops," gulped Dan. "I'm sorry. I forgot myself."

Lottie sniffed. There was a suspicious burning smell.

Something had been caught in the flames.

Can you see what has happened?

Granny's Secret

George took Dan's scaly paw. "Come on. Let's get you out of here before you do any real damage. We'll go to Granny's. She'll know what to do." They didn't have far to go as Granny Wendy lived next door.

The door opened before they could knock. "Hello Dan,"
said Granny Wendy. "I knew you were all on your way."

Dan was puzzled. How did she know they were coming?
And how did she know his name? He'd only just found out
himself. But Dan was about to discover that Granny Wendy
was no ordinary Grandma. She had an unusual secret.

Do YOU know what Granny's secret is?

The Ancient Book of Maps

Granny Wendy listened carefully to Dan's sad story and then led them to her special magic workroom. Standing on tiptoe she lifted down an old book of maps from the top shelf.

"Phoo!" she blew away the dust. "Atishoo!" the dust tickled her nose.

Granny began turning the crinkled pages. "This is the map of the Wild Westlands. Dragonland is somewhere here."

Can you find Dragonland?

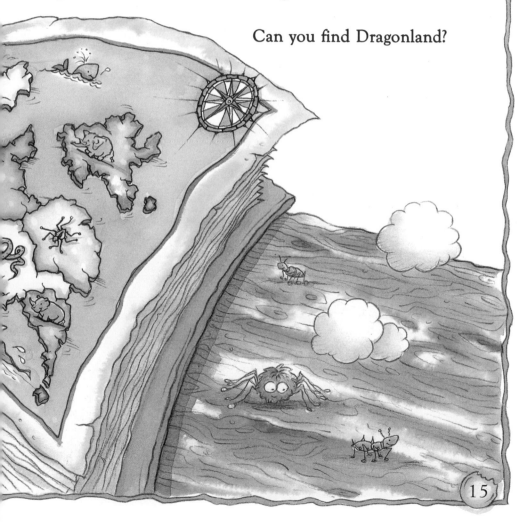

The Missing Ointment

"Where exactly do you live in Dragonland?" asked Granny. Dan looked glum. He couldn't think and his bump hurt. But Lottie had an idea. "Granny, why don't you put some of your super-duper magic yellow ointment on Dan's bump. It made my bumped knee much better last week."

Granny Wendy looked surprised. "Did it really? Well I never! I must be getting better at making lotions and potions. There's just one small problem. I don't know where it is. It's in a blue bottle with a black witch's hat on the label."

Can you find Granny's magic ointment?

17

Granny Casts a Spell

As soon as Granny rubbed the sticky yellow ointment onto his head, Dan began to look and feel better.

"I'm beginning to remember!" he squeaked, excitedly. "The place I live in is called . . . ELLIVNOGARD. "No . . . that's not exactly right. I'm afraid I'm still a bit mixed up."

George thought hard. "The word's not mixed up it's the wrong way around. I know where you live."

Do you?

Meanwhile, Granny Wendy was so encouraged by the success of her yellow ointment, that she decided to try a little more magic to help them on their way to Dragonland.

She checked the list of ingredients in her spell book. "Just a last little pinch of stardust," Granny said, smiling. "And, hey . . ." BANG!

Cave Maze

Spluttering and coughing, Dan, George, Lottie and Granny waited for the smoke to clear.

"Is this Dan's home?" asked George.

"Not quite, dear," said Granny. "Things haven't gone exactly as I planned."

"Can't you magic us out of here?" asked Lottie.

Granny looked worried. She was only halfway through the classes in her "Learn to be a Witch" course. George looked at the paths leading out of the cave.

"We don't need magic," he said. "There is one safe path out to the open air."

Which path will take them safely out of the cave?

Granny Tries Again

Back in the open, Dan's tummy rumbled loudly. He was beginning to wish he had stayed in the cupboard, at least it was full of yummy things to eat. He lay down to dream.

George and Lottie played hide-and-seek. All around they heard the sounds of birds singing and chirping. Bright, exotic butterflies flitted among the trees and flowers. In the distance, the towers and turrets of wonderful castles and palaces glinted in the sun.

Granny Wendy fumbled through her spell book.

"I've found the right spell," she said at last. "I think . . .
But I need one special flower to make it work. It has red,
bell-shaped flowers and green, diamond-shaped leaves
with yellow spots. Can you help me find it?"

George, the dragon and Lottie began the hunt.

Can you find the flower that Granny Wendy needs?

A Fantastic Flight

Clutching the flower, Granny muttered the
magic word. Silence. Nothing happened,
then suddenly: POW! FIZZZ!
Through a purple mist they saw . . .

A unicorn! It seemed to be offering them a ride. It was a tight fit, but somehow they all climbed onto his back and the creature soared into the air. The unicorn left them on a rocky crag. But something was very wrong.

This was NOT Dragonland. Lottie gulped in horror as she spotted a very fierce looking beast.

What has Lottie spotted? What country has the unicorn taken them to by mistake?

Ferocious Beasts

There was no time for another of Granny's spells. There was nowhere to hide and only one way to escape ~ down the other side of the mountain.

Lottie spotted a boat and Granny thought they could row to Dragonland in it. But first they had to find a safe path down the rocky cliff.

Can you find a safe path down to the boat?

Party Picnic

Safe at the water's edge, Granny nimbly jumped aboard the boat. But just then, a wind sprang up. They heard wings beating in the air. A tongue of flame shot past, singeing the grass. With a thud, a small dragon landed in front of them.

"We've been looking for you everywhere, Dan," the dragon exclaimed.

"It's Bess, my sister," whooped Dan.

Bess flew ahead to tell everyone that Dan was not lost anymore and by the time they arrived at Dragonville, a surprise was waiting.

A huge picnic was spread out on the grass and all Dan's family and friends were there.

"It's easy to spot my family," said Dan. "There's Ma, Pa, my sisters Bess and Izzy and brother Arthur. We all have yellow tummies and a green arrow tip at the ends of our tails."

Can you find all the dragons in Dan's family?

Home Again

Dusk was falling and the sun was setting. Even Dan's tummy was full. It was time for Granny Wendy, George and Lottie to go. Dan's Dad offered them a ride home and Dan said he would come along too. They waved goodbye to all their dragon friends and for the second time that day they soared up into the air. All too quickly, they spotted their own house below.

"But I'll see you again soon," smiled Dan. "When you hear strange noises coming from your cupboard you'll know that it's me! But next time, I'll be able to find my own way home."

Answers

Pages 6-7
This is the little dragon's story in the right order:

We went for a picnic. It became very windy. I hit a tree . . .
. . . and fell to the ground. I was dizzy and lost. I saw an open door . . .
. . . and found something to eat.

Pages 8-9
The dragon's badge is here. His name is Dan.

Pages 10-11
Dan's fiery breath has toasted the bread, boiled the milk in the mug, and singed the papers and the box of cereal. They are circled below.

Pages 12-13
Granny's secret is that she is a witch. The telltale signs are: the witch's hat, the broomstick and the spellbook, as well as the strange mix of animals in her house.

Pages 14-15
This is Dragonland.

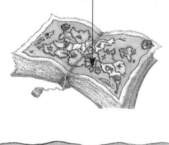

Pages 16-17
Granny's magic ointment is here.

Pages 18-19

The place where Dan lives is called DRAGONVILLE.

Pages 20-21

The safe route out of the cave is marked here.

Pages 22-23

Here is the flower that Granny needs.

Pages 24-25

Lottie has spotted a dinosaur. The unicorn has taken them to Dinosaurland by mistake.

Pages 26-27

The safe path down to the boat is marked here.

Pages 28-29

The dragons in Dan's family are circled here.

This edition first published in 2002 by Usborne Publishing Ltd., Usborne House, 83-85 Saffron Hill, London EC1N 8RT, England. www.usborne.com
Copyright © 2002, 1995 Usborne Publishing Ltd.
The name Usborne and the devices ⚲ ⊕ are Trade Marks of Usborne Publishing Ltd.
All rights reserved.